I AM READING

Yeti Spaghetti

SAMANTHA HAY

Illustrated by

MARK BEECH

MACMILLAN CHILDREN'S BOOKS

For Alice and Archie

First published 2009 by Macmillan Children's Books

This edition published 2013 by Macmillan Children's Books
a division of Macmillan Publishers Limited
20 New Wharf Road, London N1 9RR
Basingstoke and Oxford
Associated companies throughout the world
www.panmacmillan.com

ISBN 978-1-4472-0929-4

1 3 5 7 9 8 6 4 2

A CIP catalogue record for this book is available from the British Library.

Printed in China

Contents

Chapter One

4

Chapter Two

11

Chapter Three

18

Chapter Four

28

Chapter Five

32

Chapter Six

40

Chapter One

Peter was putting the final cherry on the giant jelly he was decorating when he heard a growl . . .

"Tingling tastebuds," he groaned. "The Yetis are back again!"

A big furry face was peering through the kitchen window.

"GRRRRRRR!" growled the Yeti as it reached out a long hairy hand . . .

"Hey!" yelled Peter. "STOP!"

But it was too late. The Yeti had gone.
And so had half the jelly!

Peter sighed. That was the problem
with living in the village of Scoffi: the
Yetis. A big gang of them lived on the
large snowy mountain above the
village, and every day they thundered
down into the town and made a
nuisance of themselves.

You see, Scoffi was famous for food. Everyone who lived in the village was crazy about cooking. All day they diced and sliced, and grilled and chilled, creating the most delicious dishes you've ever tasted.

The food was so fabulous that people came from far and wide to try it. And so did the Yetis.

They were everywhere: hanging around
houses and growling at windows . . .
trying to pinch titbits of whatever tasty
treats the villagers were making.

9

Peter shook his head.

It had to stop.

In two days' time it would be the annual Scoffi cookery competition and there would be chefs entering from all over the world.

Peter was hoping to be the youngest-ever winner. He was already the best cook in Scoffi. But more than anything he wanted to win the competition and prove to the world that Scoffi chefs really were the best!

The only problem was the Yetis . . .

Chapter Two

The Mayor of Scoffi called a meeting.
Everyone came – including several
Yetis, who were sniffing around the
refreshments table.

"We've got to get rid of them," said the Mayor, pointing at the Yetis. "If we can't, I'm cancelling the competition! I won't let Scoffi become the laughing stock of the world," he said crossly.

Peter sighed. His dreams of winning
the competition were sagging like
soggy sardine sandwiches.

But just then a man in a dark cloak
appeared . . .

"I believe you've got a Yeti problem,"
said the mysterious stranger.

Everyone nodded.

"Well, I might be able to help . . ."
The man whisked off his cloak to
reveal a bright green pair of shorts and
a tall hat with a huge red feather.

"I'm Yann the yodeller," he said

cheerfully.

The Mayor sighed. "That's all I need."
But before he could say another word
Yann began . . .
"YODEL-AY-EEE-OOO!"

Peter pulled a face. It sounded awful.

The Yetis didn't like it either.
They squealed and squirmed, growled
and girned,

and then ran away as fast as their big
furry legs would carry them.

It had worked. The Yetis had gone.

Chapter Three

It was competition day and all the villagers were up early, icing and slicing, chopping and wok-ing, all hoping their own dish would catch the eye of the head judge, Barry Baloney.

Peter was working hard too,

decorating a huge pineapple cake.

Proudly Peter carried his cake to the town hall, where the tables groaned with goodies. There were fabulous flans. Wonderful waffles. Lovely lasagnes. Incredible ice creams!

And right in the middle of the table
Peter placed his perfect pineapple cake.
But just then there was a mighty
CRASH and the doors of the town hall
were thrown open!

"Curdling custards!" gasped
Peter. "It's a Yeti!"
"GRRRRRRRRR!" the Yeti growled.
Everyone watched in horror.
Everyone apart from Peter, who had
spotted something rather
strange . . .

The Yeti

was carrying

a saucepan.

"ARRRGH!" screamed everyone . . .

except Peter.

Dishes were dropped, spoons were

scattered, and people dived under tables.

And then Yann appeared.

"YODEL-AY-EEE-OOO!"

24

"Hey! Stop yodelling!" shouted Peter,

whose nose had picked up a most

delicious smell coming from the Yeti's

saucepan.

But no one heard him over the noise.

"YODEL-AY-EEE-OOO!"

Peter raced over to the Yeti and peered into the saucepan. It looked like . . . "Spaghetti?" asked Peter. The Yeti nodded.

Peter's mouth watered. The spaghetti glistened like gold. The sauce was the colour of rubies. It was the most amazing spaghetti Peter had ever seen. But there was no time to admire it.

"YODEL-AY-EEE-
OOO!"

The yodelling was
too much for the Yeti.
It clutched its saucepan to its
chest and ran out of the door.

Chapter Four

Enough was enough.

Peter grabbed the first thing to hand,

which just happened to be his own perfect

pineapple cake, and flung it at Yann.

That stopped him.

"BE QUIET, ALL OF YOU!" shouted Peter.

Eventually everyone was silent.

"That Yeti wasn't dangerous," said Peter.

"Hairy bears aren't welcome here!" insisted the Mayor.

"But you don't understand," said Peter.
"I think he wants to enter our cookery
competition."

Everyone burst out laughing.

"Don't be silly!" exclaimed the Mayor.
"Yetis can't cook! Now, let's get on
with the judging."

And that was that.

Peter felt like crying.

Not only had the Yeti and his spaghetti been sent away, but Peter's perfect pineapple cake was ruined. There was no point in staying. With a heavy heart and a tear in his eye, Peter left the hall and headed home.

Chapter Five

But Peter wasn't the only one crying.

Sitting outside the town hall, sniffling

into his saucepan, was the big hairy Yeti.

Peter sat down next to him. And despite feeling glum, his tummy rumbled – the spaghetti smelt so good. The Yeti stopped sniffling and held out his saucepan to Peter.

"You want me to try it?" asked Peter hopefully.

The Yeti nodded.

Peter dipped his finger into the sauce
and tasted it.
KAZOW!

His taste buds lit up
like fairy lights.
"WOWZERS!" he
gasped. "It's delicious!"

And then suddenly an idea popped into his head.

Peter picked up the saucepan and dashed back into the hall, where the judging was nearly over.

Carefully and quietly, so that nobody
spotted him, Peter placed the saucepan
at the end of the table.

A small man appeared with an enormous spoon. It was the head judge, Barry Baloney.

He dipped his spoon into the saucepan and tasted the spaghetti.

A smile appeared on his face.

"It's good," he said.

He dipped his spoon again and tasted more. "It's *very* good," he said, smacking his lips together and grinning. "In fact, it's the best. Forget the rest. This spaghetti is the winner!"

Chapter Six

"Who created this masterpiece?" boomed the Mayor.

Peter stepped forward. "That's Yeti Spaghetti!" he said, pointing at the saucepan. "And the chef who made it is the poor Yeti you frightened away earlier."

"Did someone say Yeti?" said Yann, appearing suddenly, still covered in Peter's pineapple cake.

"Yes, I did!" said Peter sternly. "But don't even think of yodelling – or you'll get a pan of spaghetti on your head too."

Yann zipped his lips, while Barry Baloney
reached out and tasted some cake that
was clinging to the top of Yann's head.
"Mmmm," he mumbled, "delicious!" ·
And he reached for some more.
The Mayor folded his arms crossly.

"A Yeti cannot win this competition!"

"No, he can't," agreed Barry Baloney.
"Not on his own – because this cake is
tip-top too. I've decided to have two
winners: Yeti Spaghetti and this perfect
pineapple cake."

Everyone was shocked. And stunned.
And a bit put out.

But not for long. Soon the celebrations
began . . .

And the Yeti and Peter shared a big
gold cup, which they carried proudly
around the village for all to see.

ALL the Yetis turned out to be terrific cooks, which was why they'd been hanging around Scoffi bothering everyone – they were desperate to share recipes.

And Scoffi became even more famous – for its amazing Yeti chefs!

The only person who wasn't pleased was Yann – because now that the Yetis were welcome in Scoffi, yodelling was definitely off the menu.

About the Author and Illustrator

Sam Hay worked in television before escaping to Scoffi to write children's books. She lives there with her husband, two children and a Giant African Land Snail called Snaily. "I love spaghetti," says Sam, "but unfortunately I'm rubbish at cooking. But now we live in Scoffi we enjoy great grub, cooked up for us every day by the Yeti Spaghetti chef himself. Delicious!"

Mark Beech enjoys two things as much as he enjoys illustrating – yummy food and yodelling! So imagine his surprise when he discovered the town of Scoffi – truly a home from home! Mark now lives in Scoffi and can often be found drawing in the town square while eating his favourite food, Spaghetti Bolognese-flavoured ice cream, made by his Yeti friends!

Tips for Beginner Readers

1. Think about the cover and the title of the book. What do you think it will be about? While you are reading, think about what might happen next and why.

2. As you read, ask yourself if what you're reading makes sense. If it doesn't, try rereading or look at the pictures for clues.

3. If there is a word that you do not know, look carefully at the letters, sounds and word parts that you do know. Blend the sounds to read the word. Is this a word you know? Does it make sense in the sentence?

4. Think about the characters, where the story takes place, and the problems the characters in the story faced. What are the important ideas in the beginning, middle and end of the story?

5. Ask yourself questions like:
> Did you like the story?
> Why or why not?
> How did the author make it fun to read?
> How well did you understand it?

Maybe you can understand the story better if you read it again!